Jaws™* 2
Shark Tales

Jaws™* 2
Shark Tales

By Margery Altman

With pictures to color
Illustrated by Tony Tallarico

inkpot books

GROSSET & DUNLAP
A FILMWAYS COMPANY
Publishers • New York

To my "sharkest" friend, Lew.

Library of Congress catalog card number: 78-58462
ISBN: 0-448-16337-3
*JAWS™ 2 is a trademark of and licensed by
Universal City Studios, Inc.
Published simultaneously in Canada.

Printed in the United States of America.

CONTENTS

Jaws™*2
Shark Tales

Although the fishermen were scared, they had high hopes.

Monster Hunt

Would you pay $25 to meet a monster? Lots of people do. The monster is the shark—one of the most greatly feared animals in the world.

Off the coast of Montauk Point, Long Island, charter skipper Captain Frank Mundus takes adventure-seekers on monster-fishing expeditions 50 miles into the Atlantic Ocean. Many shark hunters are amateur fishermen who seldom kill a shark unless they intend to enter it for competition or eat it. For them shark-hunting is a sport.

As a conservation effort, the National Marine Fisheries Service Laboratory issues tags so that anglers may tag the sharks they catch and return them to the water. After a shark is cut loose, the hook corrodes and the giant fish survives to continue its existence as a scavenger.

In July, not too long ago, four young Long Island men became monster hunters for a day. Beginning at 7 A.M. aboard the *Cricket II*, they received early-morning advice and instructions from the experienced captain and mate. Although the fishermen were scared, they hoped to catch a shark like the one landed a few weeks before and displayed on deck. It was a 3,000-pound man-eating white shark.

The crew's routine began 4 miles offshore. The chores were boring but nevertheless necessary for a safe and successful trip. First, a wire-and-wood fish cage prepared with fresh bait was dropped into the water. Each person was given a light fishing rod with which to catch whiting for additional bait. This crew used the basic method employed by most shark fishermen, called drifting and chumming.

The boat drifted with the tide while the mate methodically dipped a small cup into a bucket of fish blood and chummed it over the side. The blood attracted the sharks to the vicinity of the boat, where they would be offered baited hooks.

Shark Waters

Realization that their boat was alone in shark-infested waters made them nervous, but by 10:30 A.M. the four adventurers were anxious for action. The captain began to prepare the boat. Belts with pole sockets and light tackle rods with lines were given to the fishermen. Hooks were baited with whiting. The mate continued the constant chumming of fish blood.

Soon the captain raised his voice. He was giving instructions to a lucky fisherman. "Strike it.

CRICKET II

"Strike it. You've got a shark there."

Catching a shark was serious business.

You've got a shark there. Now let it run. . . . The captain instructed the fisherman to let the line get tight and to keep control of the monster. Sometimes the shark would weave in and out of the water near the boat. Then its fin would be spotted 200 yards away.

Each time the shark approached the boat, the captain would try to pick up the gaff—an iron hook with which he could lift the fish out of the water. But the shark would swim away, diving down deep as if it knew what its fate would be.

The captain was no longer jolly. Catching a shark was serious business. His sharp instructions were to take the shark in a little at a time without letting the line slack. Everyone crowded on one side of the boat to watch the action. When the captain finally succeeded in hooking the shark, everyone cheered.

The shark's tail made a loud thumping noise as it struck the side of the boat. A rope was slipped over the huge tail and cranked in. Out of the water rose their amazing catch: a 7-foot blue shark.

The amateur fishermen watched in awe for a moment, unable to move. Then the captain began shouting orders again. "Come on, now. Next man up—we have to catch more than one of those today."

The next fisherman grabbed the rod and began his wait for a bite. In only fifteen minutes he had his catch, and the long process of reeling and waiting was repeated. This time the fishermen

They had been attracted by the continued chumming of
fish blood.

knew what to do. Catch number 2 was smaller than the first, but just as exciting. Four feet long and about 80 pounds in weight, it was secured to the side of the boat.

Sharks Follow Boat

In the excitement, the fishermen failed to notice that a school of sharks was recklessly swimming around the boat. They had been attracted by the continued chumming of fish blood. The men aboard were warned not to extend their arms or legs over the side.

For three hours the monster hunt continued—with ten sharks taken. The most spectacular catch was a 12-foot, 290-pound monster, after fifty-five minutes of back-breaking heaving and reeling.

As the ship pulled into the dock at Montauk, the adventurers had mixed emotions. They were relieved to have escaped the jaws of the giant fish, and also quite excited and eager to tell friends about their trip. Tourists buzzed around the boat, snapping pictures of the fishermen and their haul.

The captain bid everyone farewell and commended the fishermen on their efforts. Laughing, he invited them all back for another try. The men looked at each other and shook their heads—one monster hunt a year was excitement enough!

Patrick would meet his "friend," the shark.

Facing the Jaws

Swimming alone in the Caribbean, one is likely to meet a shark—and it may attack. But not all sharks attack, so it is possible to meet a harmless one.

Patrick Ellam did. He used to swim alone every afternoon at a quiet beach off the Caribbean island of Barbados. Equipped with a face mask, a snorkel, and a speargun, he would swim in the waters, enjoying their beauty as brightly colored fish darted in and out of the magnificent coral. And, periodically, Patrick would meet his "friend" the shark.

When he first came across the giant fish, Patrick was frightened. He realized that his speargun would be useless against the powerful creature. He knew the shark could eat him if it wished, but it didn't seem to want to.

Each time they met, the shark would swim down the beach side from the north and pass by Patrick at a distance of 20 feet. What a lovely sight. The giant fish cruised with easy, graceful movements, never changing course or letting

Patrick out of its sight. It never came any closer either. The creature was probably more curious than hungry. At least, Patrick hoped so. Although frightened, Patrick returned to swim at that very spot every day. In three or four months he and the shark got used to each other. Wondering why the shark never attacked him, Patrick did some research on the sea creatures. He thought it would be a good idea to know all he could, just in case he met an unfriendly one.

Shark Routine

Patrick learned why he and the shark always seemed to meet in the same place. Sharks commute when they can—that is, they travel back and forth, going where food is each morning and returning to their resting place in the evening. As long as the food supply lasts, they continue this routine. Their only interests seem to be eating, resting, and curiosity about things that move or shine. Sharks require lots of food, and become desperate when they can't get it. That's when most of them attack.

Patrick learned that sharks are unintelligent and unpredictable, their behavior motivated mainly by hunger and curiosity. Why, one may wonder, don't sharks, known meat-eaters, eat people more often than they do? One explanation may be that they are more timid than they seem, except when they are very hungry. Or

Patrick learned that sharks are unpredictable.

His small boat was accompanied for several hours by a
very large shark.

perhaps human beings remind sharks of octopuses, their natural enemies.

After learning about the shark's fear of octopuses, Patrick remembered a boat trip near Ceylon. His small boat was accompanied for several hours by a very large shark. However, after circling the boat constantly, the giant fish suddenly headed straight out to sea. An experienced fisherman aboard explained that the animal must have seen one of the giant octopuses that lived in the rocks below.

Advice for Swimmers

Patrick has some advice for swimmers:
1. If you are going to swim in areas where sharks have been seen, learn more about them.
2. Don't swim alone. When swimming from a boat, have someone aboard to act as a lookout.
3. Keep your head under water. Use a snorkel to breathe through and a face mask to help you see.
4. Carry an object about 3 feet long that you can use to prod a shark on the nose if it comes toward you.
5. Swim in daylight, since dim light makes visibility difficult.
6. While swimming, avoid sudden jerky movements, which might attract a shark's attention.

7. If you see a shark approaching, try not to panic. You must convince the giant fish that you are not hostile or afraid.
8. When a shark approaches, bring your weapon up in front of you, keeping it between you and the animal.
9. Do not threaten the shark.
10. Ease yourself away slowly and head toward your boat or the shore.

One Who Survived

Though sharks are the most feared fish in the oceans, not all encounters with them end in death.

During the annual South Australian Skin-diving and Spear-fishing Championship competition, in December 1963, a man named Rodney Fox was attacked by a shark. He was one person who survived to tell the tale.

A "free-diver," using no artificial breathing aids, Rodney's task was to dive for a period of five hours, spearing and bringing up fish. To win, his catch had to be the highest in total weight and include the greatest variety of fish.

An experienced underwater spearfisherman, he was among forty divers dressed in rubber suits and face masks and carrying spear-fishing guns. Each contestant also towed a hollow fish float in which to load the fish as they caught them. The containers were designed to minimize blood flowing from the speared fish, which might attract hungry sharks.

Suddenly, Rod was hit from behind.

Murky Waters

It was a bright, hot day, but the water was murky, a disadvantage for a deep-sea diver. He might have to get too close to the fish before spearing it, which would give it more time to get away.

Some time later, with only an hour and a half left in the competition, Rodney felt confident about his day's fishing. Looking at the other divers' piles of fish onshore, Rod thought he had a chance to win. He needed a few more large fish to increase the total weight of his catch.

Fish were scarce in the inshore waters by that time, so Rod moved farther out to hunt. On one of his trips he remembered spotting a group of large fish near a triangle-shaped rock. He headed in that direction to find the catch, which he was sure would put him ahead of the other divers.

As he approached the rock, Rod moved as slowly and quietly as he could, trying not to scare any fish away. Through the murky waters only about 30 feet ahead of him, Rod saw the fish. He held his spear out in front of him, ready to shoot. Then something made him stop. A sudden quiet surrounded him. He sensed that something terrible was about to happen.

Shark Attack

Suddenly, Rod was hit from behind and pushed rapidly through the water. His face mask flew off and his spear gun was knocked out of his hand. He was helpless—the prey of a giant shark!

The diver couldn't see what was happening, but he felt the monster's force all over his body as he was thrust forward. Caught in the shark's jaws, Rod tried desperately to free himself by pushing on its head.

Just as Rod thought he was free, the shark's jaws once again closed around his right arm. He fought with all his might to get loose, especially since he needed air and had to reach the water's surface.

Kicking wildly, he pushed himself above the water, having just enough time to gulp one breath of air. The shark followed close behind. In an effort to gain control of the situation, the diver wrapped his arms and legs around the shark's body, keeping away from its jaws. Down he went again, scraping the bottom. He pushed with all his strength to get loose and surface again. The shark came up after him—and for the first time Rod could see it, the great white monster that divers fear.

Escape

Rod realized that he had only a small chance of survival as the shark came toward him again. But for some reason, the shark turned before reaching him. Suddenly Rod's fish float, which was attached by a line to his belt, was being forcefully

The diver wrapped his arms and legs around the shark's body.

A boatful of friends, who were not sure of what was happening to Rod, came to his assistance.

pulled through the water. Trying frantically to release the line, Rod was being pulled with it. Miraculously, the line fell free and Rod floated to the surface, screaming "Shark!"

A boatful of friends, who were not quite sure what was happening to Rod, came to his rescue. Some men in a patrol boat lifted the diver out of the water. Handling him carefully because of his severe injuries, they reached the beach. There a police ambulance rushed him to the Royal Adelaide Hospital.

Although Rodney Fox survived the horrible incident, his body and spirit remain scarred. He still skin dives, but with much more care. He takes few risks, stays away from competition, and leaves murky waters to braver individuals. He claims that feeling a shark's jaws around a man's body once in a lifetime is frightening enough!

She noticed a pool of blood surrounding her.

Girl Meets Shark

Some people believe men are more likely to be attacked by sharks than women, though no one knows why. Some theories are that women are less exposed to sharks than men, they usually swim closer to shore, and they tend to swim in groups.

Scientists have also considered the possibility that to sharks males smell different from females. Men may exude some hormonal substance that attracts these fierce predators.

In most shark attacks the parts of the victim's body that are covered with clothing are not injured. Thus, there is little reason to believe that colors or fabrics attract sharks. Women's bright-colored bathing suits neither attract nor repel these animals.

Many instances of shark attacks on women have been reported. Some victims survived, others did not. Some stories follow.

West Palm Beach, Florida — September 21, 1931

Gertrude Holaday was swimming at a public beach about 200 feet off shore. It was a warm, pleasant day. Miss Holaday looked up for just a moment to observe the beach activity. When she turned, she saw a "huge fish." At the same time she noticed a pool of blood surrounding her. Without realizing it, she had already been bitten by an 8-foot hammerhead shark.

Screaming loudly for help, she kept moving rapidly to get away from the shark. Sam Barrows, the lifeguard on duty at the beach, grabbed some life-saving equipment and swam out to help Miss Holaday. He safely brought her back to shore, the shark following closely behind them.

Miss Holaday was rushed to a nearby hospital, where she was treated for several shark bites and skin lacerations. She survived and recovered completely from her injuries.

Margate, South Africa — December 30, 1957

About 30 yards from shore, Julia Painting was taking a cooling dip in the clear calm sea. The fifteen-year-old girl was only a few feet away from a crowd of people when a large shark came in to attack. Julia screamed, trying to escape from its grip. Her friend, Paul Brokensha, came to her aid, punching at the shark and trying to force it to let go of the girl. The impact of the shark's

Her friend came to her aid.

The girl was already dead.

movement was so great that Paul was knocked away by its tail. Finally it lost interest in the battle and swam away.

Despite many bystanders' fears that Julia might already be dead, she was rushed to the hospital, where she was treated and eventually released on January 17th—not without serious scars from her unfortunate episode.

Red Sea, near the Gulf of Aqaba—April 1968

Captain Ted Falcon-Barker and his crew were on an exploratory expedition of the waters beneath the Mediterranean sea. An experienced sailor on a well-equipped vessel, the *Pagan III*, the captain and his companions were constantly on guard against shark attacks.

Jill Reed, a staff member on a women's magazine and an experienced diver, was one of the eleven divers on the trip. The ship had been sailing for several weeks when it was nearing some small islands in the Red Sea near the Gulf of Aqaba. This area was known to be filled with sharks, but it was also an ideal place for the crew to conduct some of its experiments.

One morning Jill dived off the boat to investigate the area. A few seconds later, she returned, flying back up the ladder and screaming with terror. She had met a shark. Her shoulder was bleeding. A large piece was bitten out of one of her flippers, and the top of her wet suit was torn as the shark's sandpaperlike skin brushed against her. Though Jill was used to exploring dangerous and unknown waters, she and the crew were shaken by the close call.

**Oakura Beach, Taranaki,
New Zealand — January 8, 1966**

Rae Marion Keightley was not as fortunate as the women just described. The 14-year-old high school student was dead by the time she reached the beach.

She had been swimming about 100 yards offshore with some friends and a surfboard. Unnoticed, a shark sneaked up to the group and attacked Miss Keightley. Most of the swimmers scurried to the shore. Eighteen-year-old Anthony Johns paddled over to the victim on his surfboard and pushed her onto it. Then two small waves caught the surfboard and washed the two ahore. The girl was already dead.

The Man With the
Anti-Shark Gun

There are some defenses against sharks. Experienced diver Scott G. Slaughter knows "you can't accurately predict the behavior of *any* shark," but he has developed his own weapons against them.

His own war against sharks began in 1957, when he was twenty. Spear-fishing off the coast of Hawaii, he found himself competing with a shark for a parrot fish he had just speared. The shark pushed against Scott's back, moved upward between his shoulders, and took the fish. Scott was lucky to return to his boat unharmed.

Disliking the odds against him, Scott decided to increase his chances to win an argument with the next shark he met. He began investigating underwater weapons, and learned about the powerhead invented by a man named Charles Alexander.

The weapon's gunlike mechanism consisted of a sliding metal tube holding a .45-caliber cartridge. This apparatus could be attached to the

The diver was angry!

diver's usual spear shaft. As the spear was pushed up against a shark, a firing pin released a shot, wounding the fish and releasing toxic gases. This weapon was very effective against sharks at close range.

Adapts Gun

Slaughter adapted this special gun and first tried it out in March 1957. Fishing on a Florida reef with some marine buddies, he spotted a 20-pound snapper in the clear waters. Diving off the boat, Scott got close enough to spear the fish. As he began surfacing, he spotted a huge black-tip shark circling him and eyeing his catch. Then the black-tip lunged forward and bit the fish, cutting it into two. Not only did it steal a great catch, but it also damaged Scott's spear. The diver was angry! He swam to the boat, grabbed the power-head, and dived back into the water to search for the hated shark. As the diver had expected, the shark came right up to his bait. It was opening its mouth to devour the bait when Scott aimed his powerhead right between its eyes. BOOM! The shark stopped, stiffened, and then sank to the bottom. Landing on its side, it didn't move again.

Scott was satisfied. He had proved that the powerhead was an effective anti-shark weapon.

By the fall of 1957, the shark hunter had succeeded in killing seven or eight sharks and was proud of his ability at the sport. But then Scott met the shark that almost won.

Close Call

He and Rudy Enders were diving about 25 miles from Key West. Going down to retrieve some bait that had fallen from their boat, Scott encountered an enormous white shark. Surfacing quickly, he returned to the boat for his powerhead, and dived back down. As he drew near he saw a giant shark gulp down a 3-foot grouper fish. Approaching the shark from above and behind, Scott thrust the powerhead toward the center of its head. But the shark was moving too rapidly and the shot missed, hitting it in the right eye.

The shark began thrashing about. Scott reloaded his weapon, just in case. He went back in with his powerhead to finish off the animal. By that time it had regained its senses and the shark lunged toward Scott, who dived for the bottom to keep out of its sight. The shark kept turning and moving toward him until it had maneuvered itself right in front of Scott. Then it opened its mouth wide enough to swallow the man.

Acting quickly, the diver sensed that he must move upward. At just the right moment, Scott drove his weapon against the top of the shark's head. The shot exploded and the shark sank to the bottom.

Scott had just enough time to turn over and hit the shark
with the powerhead.

Scott returned to his boat and after calming his nerves, he and Rudy dived below to examine the conquest. A hole the size of a grapefruit was in the roof of the shark's mouth. With difficulty they measured the giant fish in relation to their 7-foot boat. Its tail extended far beyond the stern. The two experienced divers guessed that the shark must have weighed between two and three thouand pounds. The shark's stomach was empty, indicating that the fish must have been hungry.

Weapon Fails

A few days later, the diver had another close call. He hit a sand shark in the head with his powerhead, and the cartridge failed to explode. Luckily, the sand shark wasn't interested in a battle and swam away. Scott couldn't help wondering what might have happened if the fish had been a hungry white shark.

Most of Scott's battles with sharks were to keep the fish he caught, but once he was attacked by a shark for no apparent reason. While he was spearfishing off Coalbin Rock, a large grouper fish he planned to use as bait got caught in a cave. Scott tried unsuccessfully to free it. He surfaced and entered his boat to get a knife and—just in case—his powerhead. It was lucky he did! Just as he dived back into the water, a tremendous white shark came at him head-on. As it opened its jaws, Scott had just enough time to turn over and hit it with the powerhead. The shark sank to the bottom and Scott escaped again.

In spite of his close calls, Scott Slaughter continues to dive and develop new, more powerful weapons. He also gains more confidence in his war against sharks. One day, he says, he might even challenge a killer whale.

The swimmers had to wait in shark-infested waters.

Sharks Face New Weapons

Many scientists and laymen believe all sharks are unpredictable. Humans know relatively little about the behavior patterns of these animals, the environmental conditions that encourage them to attack, or what provokes attacks.

The war against dangerous sharks continues, and with it comes the invention of anti-shark weapons. The United States Navy has been responsible for the development of several new devices to protect people in Naval operations.

In July 1971, a new anti-shark weapon was used to aid Navy swimmers assigned to pick up Apollo 15 astronauts after their splash-down in the Pacific Ocean.

The swimmers had to wait in shark-infested waters for several hours until the space capsule landed. Upon its arrival, the men had to attach a flotation collar to keep the space capsule from overturning or floating away. At the same time, the astronauts were lifted from the water by helicopter and taken to the deck of a waiting ship.

Anti-Shark Syringe

Although sharks don't usually attack men without provocation, the Navy wasn't taking any chances. The men were armed with a new weapon, a giant syringe. When this object was jabbed against a shark's belly, the needle penetrated the hide and injected the shark with carbon dioxide. Unable to swim or breathe, the shark couldn't bother the divers.

The Navy did not create the weapon because it was interested in killing or catching sharks, but to protect people from shark attack.

The Dart

Another Navy invention, in December 1971, was the dart. The electronic dart, which received a U.S. Patent, protected divers by overpowering sharks. Clarence G. Blanc, a member of the staff of the Naval Undersea Research and Development Center in Pasadena, California, was responsible for the invention.

The dart was a bladelike electrode that could be fired into a shark with a spear gun. The system ran on batteries, creating an electric current through the shark and in the water. It entered the shark's body, completing an electric current connected to another electrode in the water. The current, which was turned on and off at regular intervals much like the pulse of a beating heart, kept the shark powerless and enabled divers to complete their work.

The Navy wasn't taking any chances.

It kept the shark powerless and enabled divers to complete their work.

Little of the bag or the victim would show above the water.

The Navy claimed that this anti-shark device was effectively used in several instances when Navy divers were investigating air and sea wrecks.

Shark Screen

An assistant department head at the Naval Undersea Center in San Diego, California, received a U.S. Patent for another anti-shark invention. Designed to protect survivors of air and sea disasters, it was a screen in which a person could enfold himself to avoid attracting sharks. The device was vacuum-packed in a package the size of a cigarette box and could be carried in a shirt pocket.

After unfolding the bag and filling it with water, the disaster victim could crawl safely inside. An inflated collar at the top would keep the cone-shaped bag floating upright. The bag's outer surface would be free from bulges that might attract sharks. The top of the bag could be closed by pulling a drawstring inside. Little of the bag or the victim would show above the water.

The protective bag was made of a black, thin material like mylar. Its surface was coated with an aluminizing layer, which acted as a radar reflector. Thus the victim was protected from sharks, and easier to sight in rescue efforts.

Although this protective device was not used often, it effectively protected survivors and gave them a somewhat greater feeling of safety.

Enclosing Nixon's private beach were wire nets treated with shark repellent.

Protecting Key Biscayne

In August 1970, soon after President Richard Nixon purchased his retreat at Key Biscayne, Florida, efforts were made to protect the property from sharks.

Enclosing Nixon's private beach were wire nets treated with shark repellent. A few days after the nets had been set up, trappers for the local seaquarium pulled six big snapping tiger sharks out of the water near Nixon's home. Local authorities repeatedly maintained that shark attacks had never been reported in that area. But it was better to be safe then sorry.

Although there was no official record of shark attack on the bay side of Key Biscayne, where the President's home was located, fear was still rampant among local inhabitants. Florida, it happens, leads all states in shark disasters. The Navy's shark-attack file lists an average of four to five fully documented shark attacks every year in that state.

Nets may have been set up on President Nixon's beach because of the disappearance in 1968 of Australian Prime Minister Harold Holt. Holt was presumed to have been devoured by sharks while skin diving in the water near his summer home at Portsea on Australia's southern coast.

Sharklore:
Myths and Legends From Ancient Times and Other Lands

Sharks have been the subjects of stories for thousands of years. Ancient peoples from different lands told tales about these sea monsters, which have been passed on through the years as myths and legends.

Unlike present-day stories, legends did not always depict sharks as man's enemy. Sometimes sharks acted as guides directing lost ships towards shore without harming the sailors.

Dead Ancestors

A South Sea sailor and his wife were frightened when a giant shark jumped out of the water and into their canoe. The man's first impulse was to kill it with his spear. But as the shark looked into his eyes, the sailor was overcome by a magic spell. Overturning the canoe to

The man's first impulse was to kill it.

free the shark, the man and his wife calmly watched it swim away.

This story derives from the legend that there were two kinds of sharks in the South Seas. One was the giant fish known to be a killer. The other was a dead person who had returned to life in the form of a shark, or a living person who could transform himself to a shark. When the South Seas sailor looked into the eyes of the shark, he was reminded of one of his parents.

Most legends portray the shark as a creature to be feared. Ancient sailors were superstitious and believed it was a sign of bad luck to encounter a shark in the oceans. It was traditional on French ships to ward off the evil by nailing the tail of a shark to the bow. Without it, sailors did not feel safe at sea.

Some sailors believed sharks followed ships to eat the galley garbage thrown overboard. But others believed a shark could sense the approaching death of a man. Despite attempts to scare off the evil fish, sharks stayed close to ships aboard which an epidemic of yellow fever or cholera broke out. As the sailors died, they were buried at sea—and eaten by sharks.

Scottish Legends

Legends from Scotland show that sharks were disliked as much as witches. When these sea creatures followed ships, the sailors aboard viewed it as a sure sign of death. Sailors on one vessel that was pursued made several attempts to get rid of the shark. Finally, after it attacked a crew member, an officer devised a plan to destroy the animal.

From the ship's kitchen he brought the hide of a pig. From the sailmaker, he obtained a canvas pouch, which he partially filled with sand. Then the smith heated a small cannonball until it was red hot. Some fresh blood was dropped overboard to attract the shark. Meanwhile, the crew prepared the pig hide. They put the hot cannonball in the pouch and sewed the pouch into the pig hide. Then it was thrown to the hungry shark, which devoured it in one gulp. A moment later the shark began to swim faster. Then it jumped out of the water and onto the shore. A few crew members who rowed to the beach found that the cannonball had burned a hole in the shark's belly.

Primitive Beliefs

Primitive men believed constellations of stars in the sky symbolized their own struggles with what they considered a devil god—the shark. The greek constellation we know as Orion's belt was believed to be the missing leg of Nohi-Abassi by the Warrau Indians of South America. Nohi-Abassi, a Warrau tribesman, had thrown his mother-in-law to a shark. To punish Nohi-

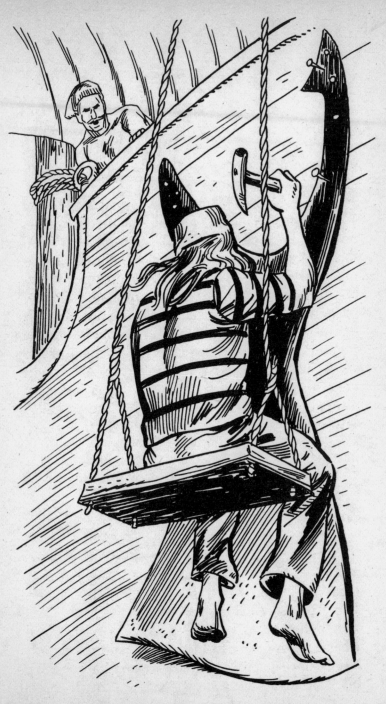

It was traditional to ward off the evil by nailing the tail of a
shark to the bow.

As the sailors died, they were buried at sea.

Abassi, his sister-in-law, acting as a shark, cut off his leg.

Shark worship was not uncommon in primitive religions. The shark-gods demanded human sacrifice. In some islands, a priest randomly selected people—men, women, and children—to be thrown to the sharks. On other islands caves were built near the shore. After ceremonial rites were performed, human bodies were placed on stones in front of the caves as gifts for the shark-gods.

Ancient Hawaiian tapestries depict stories about sharks. One is the story of Kamo-hoa-lii, the king of the sharks. In the legend he transformed himself into a man, married a fair maiden, and fathered a child. Nanaie, Kamo-hoa-lii's child, possessed the magical power to transform himself into a shark. In that form, he ate many island people. The fearsome shark was captured, killed, and taken to a sacred hill in Kain-alu. There, the enraged villagers cut up the body of the shark-man with pieces of bamboo. This angered the gods. To this day the bamboo that grows on the hill in Kain-alu is blunt, not sharp like bamboo on other parts of the island.

Test of Strength

As a test of strength, Hawaiian warriors entered shark pens and fought the sharks. Using only a shark-tooth sword as a weapon, a shark-warrior faced a single life-or-death combat. A

It jumped out of the water and onto the shore.

warrior who won was believed to possess magical powers.

Hawaiian women wore tattoos on their ankles to protect themselves from shark bites. The tattoos represented ancient warriors who had been bitten by sharks and survived.

Shark Charmers

In the Fiji Islands, there are legends about charming sharks in the same way that snakes are charmed. A priest, Father Laplante, claimed to have seen islanders subdue sharks by kissing them. He attributed this feat to magical powers, reporting that after a native kissed a shark it did not move. Natives held several shark-kissing ceremonies annually to keep the sharks away.

Sharklore

Although most sharklore portrays sharks as evil, dreaded sea creatures, ships have often been named *Shark*, perhaps as a tribute to these animals' power and mastery of the seas. A famous American sailor, Commodore Matthew Perry, commanded the *Shark* and took possession of a well-known shark-fishing spot in Florida.

Literature and art include references to these sea creatures. Sharks appear as symbols in

The warrior faced a single life-or-death combat.

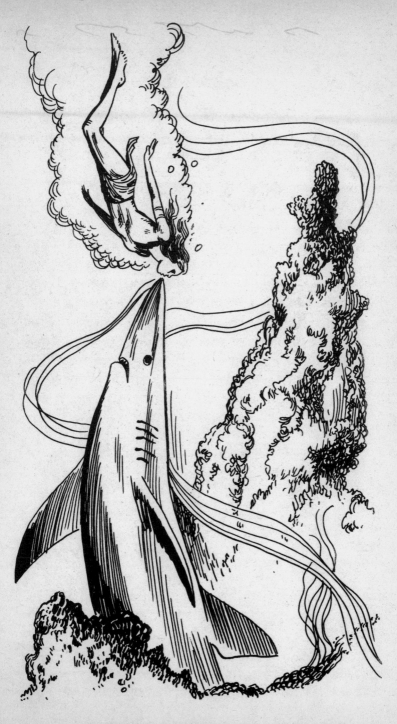

Islanders subdued sharks by kissing them.

British coats-of-arms and in famous early paint-
ings. In Shakespeare's famous play, *Macbeth*, the
recipe for Witch's stew includes:

> "Scale of dragon, tooth of wolf,
> Witches' mummy, maw and gulf
> Of the ravin'd salt-sea shark."

  Many things have changed through the cen-
turies, but one constant has been man's ambiva-
lent attitude toward sharks. He is both fascinated
by and terrified of that awesome sea creature—
and with good reason.